Leo and Aaron rushed over to where a black-and-white Collie dog was chewing on a rubber bone. His tail wagged happily as they looked at him. Next to him was a short, fat white dog with a patch on one side.

"There's a dog over there that's hairier than Dad!" Leo laughed.

Zoe followed her family as they looked from dog to dog. Then, amongst all the other noises, she heard a small bark: "*Rruff! Rruff, rruff!*" over and over again. Zoe stepped away from everyone else, and tried to work out where it was coming from. She looked all around, but none of the dogs nearby seemed to be barking. "*Rruff. Rruff, rruff, RRUFF!*" she heard again. She followed the sound down the hallway and up to a kennel in the corner. Inside was the teeniest, tiniest little brown-and-white puppy!

"*Rruff!*" he said as he looked at her happily.

Have you read all these books in the
Battersea Dogs & Cats Home series?

PIPPIN'S
story

by
Sarah Hawkins

Illustrated by Artful Doodlers
Puzzle illustrations by Jason Chapman

RED FOX

BATTERSEA DOGS & CATS HOME: PIPPIN'S STORY
A RED FOX BOOK 978 1 782 95046 2

First published in Great Britain by Red Fox,
an imprint of Random House Children's Publishers
A Random House Group Company

This edition published 2013

1 3 5 7 9 10 8 6 4 2

The Random House Group Limited supports the Forest Stewardship
Council® (FSC®), the leading international forest-certification organisation.
Our books carrying the FSC label are printed on FSC®-certified paper. FSC is
the only forest-certification scheme supported by the leading environmental
organisations, including Greenpeace. Our paper procurement policy can be
found at www.randomhouse.co.uk/environment.

MIX
Paper from
responsible sources
FSC® C016897

Set in 13/20 Stone Informal

Red Fox Books are published by Random House Children's Publishers,
61–63 Uxbridge Road, London W5 5SA

www.**randomhousechildrens**.co.uk
www.**randomhouse**.co.uk

Address .... The Random House Group Limited .... ted

.... The Random House Group Limited Reg. No. 954009

A CIP catalogue .... record for this book is available from the British Library.

.... Printed and bound in Great Britain by
.... CPI Group (UK) Ltd, Croydon CR0 4YY

Turn to page 91 for lots
of information on
Battersea Dogs & Cats Home,
plus some cool activities!

Meet the stars of the Battersea Dogs & Cats Home series to date . . .

Bailey

Chester

Misty

Max

Daisy

Rusty

Snowy

Huey

Stella

Angel

Alfie

Cosmo

Buddy and Holly

Coco

Petal

Suzy

Jessie

Bertie

Oscar

Bruno

Sparkle and Belle

Buster

Pippin

A Brilliant School Trip!

Zoe jumped up and down impatiently as Mum packed her lunchbox. "Calm down!" Mum laughed.

"I'm too excited!" Zoe grinned.

"About what?" her big brother Aaron asked as he came into the kitchen and grabbed a piece of toast from her plate.

"Oi!" Zoe complained. Her even bigger brother Leo, a sleepy-looking teenager, followed Aaron into the kitchen and went to look in the fridge. Like Zoe, they both had chocolate-coloured skin, curly hair and brown eyes, but they were much taller and louder than she was.

Aaron opened his mouth so she could see all the gross mushed-up toast inside.

Zoe ignored her brother and started playing with her plaited hair. "I was talking about my school trip. The best thing," she said loudly, "is that while I'm at a brilliant theme park, you two will be in lessons." Zoe turned to Aaron and stuck her tongue out.

"So when you're in Maths, I'll be on a rollercoaster. *Ner ner-ner ner ner!*"

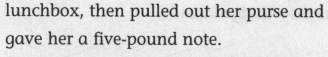

"Here," said Mum as she handed her the lunchbox, then pulled out her purse and gave her a five-pound note.

"Wow, thanks, Mum!" Zoe gasped.

"Hey!" Aaron cried as he saw the money.

"You had the same when you went on your Year Three school trip," Mum said. "I seem to remember that you spent the whole five pounds on blue and red slushy drinks, and then were sick on the rollercoaster."

"Oh yeah," Aaron laughed. "Purple puke! That was wicked."

"Boys are gross." Zoe shook her head.

The coach was waiting in the playground when Mum dropped them off at school, and Zoe could see her best friend Maya waving through the window. "Have fun in your lessons!" Zoe teased her brothers as they trudged inside.

"I saved us good seats!" Maya yelled
when Zoe climbed on board. As Zoe
walked down the aisle, her foot caught
on something and she stumbled. She
looked back to see horrid Mark Johnson
grinning at her. He'd put his foot out to
trip her on purpose.

"Oh, ha ha," Zoe said, trying to sound
normal even though she could feel her
face going red.

"Sorry, didn't see you
there," Mark said
in a voice that
meant he wasn't
sorry at all.
"Must be
because
you're
soooooooo
small."

His friends laughed and Zoe felt herself blush. She was the smallest in her class, but she'd never worried about it until Mark started picking on her. She barely came up to Maya's shoulders and it didn't matter to her at all.

"Just ignore him," Maya said as Zoe slipped into the seat next to her.

"I will," Zoe grinned. "Not even Mark is going to ruin our fun today!"

Zoe and Maya and their friends Kate and Lily spent the journey chatting excitedly about all the rides they were going to go on. "We came here for my sister's birthday," Kate said.

"The big water flume is
so much fun. You go
in these little
wooden boats and
go down really
fast and splash at
the bottom."

"I want to go on the
one where you get to float around in a
rubber ring," Maya said, flicking her
curly red hair out of her eyes. "They blow
bubbles at you, and it's so pretty."

"We can do all of them!" Zoe said.
"We've got all day, and it's going to be *so*
much fun!"

Zoe felt even more excited when they
pulled up at the park. Mark and his
friends had been noisily singing "Ten
Green Bottles" for ages and she couldn't
wait to get out of the coach.

One of the teachers handed them all tickets, counted their heads and led them through the turnstiles. "Stay in your groups, and we'll meet back here for lunch at one p.m.," she yelled over the growing chatter. "Have fun!"

Zoe looked around in amazement at all the rides. "There's the flume!" Kate shrieked, pointing to where a watery rollercoaster twisted and turned down a mountain. Zoe felt a bubble of excitement as she heard happy screams

coming from the people who were
splashing down into the water. There was
already a huge queue winding up to the
doors, and the girls rushed over to join it.

A sign next to the queue said the
waiting time was fifteen minutes, but
with everyone chatting to each other it
didn't feel long at all. Zoe, Maya, Kate
and Lily got more and more excited as
they shuffled closer to the start. Soon
there was only one family ahead of them.

"Next!" a man wearing a blue uniform yelled when they finally got to the front. He looked at the girls, then stared at Zoe. "Come here, young lady," he said in a bored voice. Zoe shrugged at her friends as she stepped out of the queue. The man pointed at a plastic cartoon dolphin with its flipper sticking out. "You've got to be taller than this to go on the ride," he muttered.

Zoe felt her face go hot with embarrassment. She could feel everyone watching her.

"Come on, love, I haven't got all day," the ride attendant snapped.

Zoe walked up to the stupid dolphin and stood up against it. The flipper was just above her head. She was too small to go on the ride.

A Small Problem

As Zoe struggled not to cry, there was a laugh from behind her in the queue. She looked up to see Mark there with his friends, Alex and Ben.

"Look at Zoe!" he sniggered. "Sorry, they don't let babies on rollercoasters! Why don't you go and find the children's play area?" His friends all laughed like he'd said something really clever.

"Stop it!" Maya yelled at Mark, then turned to Zoe, her face full of sympathy. "This is so unfair."

"Sorry, miss, it's the rules," the attendant said to Zoe, pointing her away from the queue. "It's for your own safety."

Zoe felt like she was going to cry. She tried to hold in her tears and smile at the others. "You guys go," she said.

"Not without you." Maya crossed her arms and scowled at the attendant.

"Let's find another ride to go on instead," Kate said, looking up longingly at the mountain.

"No! You have to go!" Zoe gave Maya a little push towards the log car. "I'll just wait until you come down, then we'll all go on the next one together. There must be some rides for babies like me," she tried to joke.

Maya gave her a fierce hug. "You're *not* a baby," she said.

"Go!" Zoe told her.

"We'll be really quick," Maya promised. "We'll meet you at the gift shop by the start of the queue."

Zoe nodded, not trusting herself to speak as the others climbed into the log car and the attendant strapped them in.

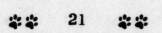

She walked slowly back past all the people in the queue, her face burning with embarrassment. All of them would know she was too much of a baby to go on the ride. Finally she came to the gift shop. She looked around at all the people bustling past her, having fun.

Maybe I can get something with my pocket money? she thought as she went inside the shop. There were all kinds of things – toys and pens, pencils and notepads, but everything had the stupid cartoon dolphin on. Zoe looked at his big smiling face and felt like he was laughing at her.

She turned to go, but just as she was leaving she spotted a stand full of soft toy animals. There were huge monkeys and lions, dogs and cats and dolphins in every single colour she could think of.

"This one, Mummy!" a little boy called as he ran up to the display and picked out a large gorilla in a blue T-shirt. As he pulled it out, a tiny toy fell to the floor, but he didn't notice. He hugged the gorilla to his chest and looked up at his mum pleadingly. "Please!"

"OK," his mum laughed.

As they walked off, Zoe went over to pick the little toy up. It was a tiny black dog with floppy ears. Zoe looked at the price tag. It said five pounds, all her spending money, but she couldn't bear to leave him all on his own in the shop.

"We tiny things have to stick together," she told him, rubbing his soft fur against her face.

Zoe sat outside the shop with her new toy until the others came and found her. They were soaked and laughing about how the water had splashed them. "Lily pulled such a funny face – it was like this!" Maya showed Zoe.

"How could you see?" Kate laughed. "Maya had her eyes shut the whole time!" she explained.

Zoe showed them all her toy puppy and they crowded around to admire him.

"He's so cute!" Maya said, stroking his fur. "You'll have to call him Patch," she added, tracing the brown splodge over his eye.

"Patch," Zoe muttered to herself. "That's a lovely name. Patch is coming on the next ride," she told the others, crossing her fingers tightly. "And so am I!"

A Big Surprise!

"How was everyone's day?" Dad asked that evening as the family crowded noisily around the kitchen table. Zoe's brothers both started telling him what they'd been doing.

Aaron grinned. "We had football, it was wicked."

"Yeah, until you kicked the ball over the fence," Leo laughed.

"Did not." Aaron shoved his brother.

"Save some for Zoe!" Mum called as Aaron started piling potatoes onto his plate.

"I'm a growing boy," Aaron said cheekily.

"I'm growing too!" Zoe protested.

Aaron laughed. "No you're not, mouse. You're going to be a teeny tiny little mouse for ever."

"I'm not a mouse!" Zoe complained.

"Then why are you so small?" Leo teased. Aaron gave him a high-five and they both laughed.

Zoe felt her cheeks go red and hot.

"Hey, that's enough of that," Mum said firmly. "Good things come in small packages, you know."

But Zoe slammed her knife and fork down and glared at her brothers. "I'm SICK of being teased, OK?"

"OK, OK," Leo said, looking shocked.

"Sorry, sis," Aaron muttered.

Zoe looked at her brothers' faces and

felt bad. It wasn't them she was cross at, really.

"What's wrong?" Mum asked. "Did something happen at the theme park?"

Zoe gave a deep sigh and clutched Patch tightly. "I wasn't tall enough to go on the big rides," she said sadly.

"Oh, Zoe!" Mum said sympathetically.

"It's not fair!" Zoe cried. "Being small is ruining everything! I wish I could grow!"

"You will!" Mum told her. "And anyway, there's nothing wrong with being short."

Zoe wasn't convinced. She felt her thumb sneak into her mouth, the way it always did when she was tired or sad. *Maybe Mark is right*, she thought, a tear trickling down her cheek. *Maybe I am a baby.*

"Come here, Pumpkin," Dad said, patting his lap. Zoe climbed up and looped her arm around his neck to give him a big hug.

"You are perfect just the way you are," Dad said, wiping her tears away. He looked at Mum and smiled widely. "I think Zoe needs some good news to cheer her up," he said.

Mum gave a secretive smile. "I think you might be right!"

"What?" Aaron started jiggling up and down. "What?"

"What would you like more than anything in the world?" Dad asked.

"A motorbike," Leo said.

"No chance," Mum snorted.

"A pet!" Aaron yelled.

"Yes, a puppy!" Zoe said, holding up Patch. "A *real* one," she added hastily.

Dad and Mum shared a big grin. "Well, we were thinking that maybe you were old enough – and big enough" – Mum looked at Zoe – "to help us look after a dog."

Zoe's thumb came out of her mouth with a *pop*! Aaron jumped up and started running around the table.

"Really?" Zoe gasped. "Really truly?"
She hugged Dad with excitement.

"Cool!" Leo beamed.

"I'll be at home with him during the
day," Mum said, "but you'll all need to
help with taking him for walks and
looking after him."

"We will," Zoe promised. She'd do
anything if it meant she could have a
dog of her own!

"What type of dog will it be?" Aaron
asked excitedly.

"That's up to you," Mum smiled.
"We're going to get it from
Battersea Dogs & Cats Home
in a couple of weeks. Do
you know what the
Home is?"

Zoe shook her
head.

"It's a place where they look after cats and dogs that don't have anywhere to live," Dad explained. "They make sure that they're all right, and then they find them a family of their own to live with."

"That's so nice!" Zoe said. "Hear that, Patch?" She lifted her puppy up to her face and squeezed him tight. "We're getting a new friend!"

Battersea Dogs & Cats Home

In the car, Zoe could barely contain her excitement. Aaron put in his headphones so he could listen to music, but Zoe started drawing a picture in her notebook. A head, a round body, four legs, little ears, and a waggly tail! She didn't know what her dog looked like yet, but she would soon. They were on their way to Battersea Dogs & Cats Home and

Zoe was going to meet her puppy!

By the time they parked the car, Zoe's notebook was filled with pictures of dogs. There was one with a long tail and one with a short tail, one with floppy ears

and another with small, triangular ears. But they were all big dogs.

"Didn't you draw any little ones?" Mum asked as Zoe and the boys got out and Dad went to buy a parking ticket.

"No, because being small is rubbish," Zoe said. "Is someone bullying you?" Mum looked down at Zoe seriously. "Is that why you're so upset about your size all of 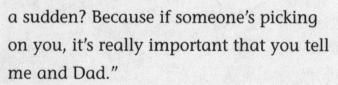 a sudden? Because if someone's picking on you, it's really important that you tell me and Dad."

"Yeah," Leo told her. "No one picks on our sister 'cept us."

Zoe shook her head. "It's OK. There's just a boy at school who says mean things sometimes. He says I'm a baby."

Mum looked very cross. "Well, that shows what he knows. You can't tell what someone's like because of their size, or what they look like at all. It's what people *do* that matters – and what this boy is doing is being very mean and silly. If you ask me, *he's* the baby."

Zoe giggled.

"But, if it gets any worse, you have to tell me, OK, sweetheart?" Mum kissed her forehead.

"I will, I promise," Zoe said. "But I'm not sad, Mum. I don't think I'll ever be sad again now that I'm going to have a puppy of my very own!"

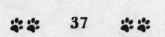

*

"If you'd like to wait in the interview room," the lady at the Battersea Dogs & Cats Home reception said, "Mandy will come and see you in a minute."

Everyone bundled into the little room. There were only two chairs, so Aaron and Leo sat on the floor, while Zoe perched on Mum's lap. She felt her thumb creeping into her mouth again as she waited for Mandy to arrive. *What if they said she wasn't old enough to have a dog?*

But when a lady
came into the room,
Zoe felt better
straight away. She
had a dark brown
bob and glasses,
and a blue
Battersea Dogs &
Cats Home jumper
that was covered in
lots of yellow fur.

Mandy wiped her
hands on her jeans and shook hands
with Mum and Dad. "Sorry to keep you
waiting. I was playing with Benji, one of
our Golden Retrievers," she explained.
"He didn't want me to go!" She looked at
Zoe and smiled. "So you want a dog of
your own?" she asked. Zoe put her thumb
back in her mouth and nodded.

Mandy asked a few questions about the size of their house and garden, and then looked at them seriously.

"Having a dog is like having another member of the family – another brother or sister," she said to Zoe and the boys. "It's not a toy that you can stop playing with when you get bored."

Zoe nodded fiercely. She was surprised to see that even her brothers looked serious for once. "We're going to be really, really good dog owners," she told Mandy.

"We'll take him for lots of walks," Leo promised.

"And teach him tricks," Aaron said.

"And give him lots and lots of love," Zoe added. "That's the most important thing."

Mum gave an approving nod and kissed the top of her head.

Mandy gave them a big smile. "It certainly is. Well, it sounds like you'll be very good dog owners. Any of our dogs would be lucky to go to such a loving home." She stood up and clapped her hands. "Let's go and find your puppy!"

Zoe felt even more excited than she'd been at the theme park, more excited than she'd ever been in her whole life, as she followed Mandy through a blue door

and up a slope, past a long row of
kennels with a dog in each one.

"Have a look around," Mandy told
them, "and let me know if you have any
questions."

Leo and Aaron rushed over
to where a black-
and-white Collie
dog was
chewing on a
rubber bone.
His tail wagged
happily as they
looked at him.
Next to him was
a short, fat white
dog with a patch on
one side.

"There's a dog over there that's hairier
than Dad!" Leo laughed.

Zoe followed her family as they looked from dog to dog. Then, amongst all the other noises, she heard a small bark: "*Rruff! Rruff, rruff!*" over and over again. Zoe stepped away from everyone else, and tried to work out where it was coming from. She looked all around, but none of the dogs nearby seemed to be barking. "*Rruff. Rruff, rruff, RRUFF!*" she heard again. She followed the sound down the hallway and up to a kennel in the corner. Inside was the teeniest, tiniest little brown-and-white puppy!

"*Rruff!*" he said as he looked at her happily.

Pippin

Zoe stared down at the little puppy. He put
his front paws against the cage and
stretched up as far as he could, his tiny
tail wagging hard. He was brown and
white, with brown ears and a white stripe
down his nose. His body was plump and
podgy and he had ears like floppy
triangles that looked like the softest velvet.

"Mum, Dad, everyone! Come over
here," Zoe called. "Look!"

She stood up, and the puppy barked and started jumping up and down as if he was saying "Don't go!"

Mum and Dad came over with Mandy. "That's Pippin," Mandy said. "Do you want to take him outside for a run around?"

"*Rruff!*" Pippin barked excitedly.

Everyone laughed.

"Oh, yes *please*," Zoe breathed. Mandy went inside the kennel, but as she was reaching down to attach the lead to his collar, Pippin shot out between her legs and raced straight towards Zoe!

Zoe dropped to her knees and Pippin ran all the way around her, then jumped up at her legs, trying to get his whole body stroked at once.

"He's so funny!" Zoe giggled.

While Zoe petted Pippin, Mandy managed to hook the lead onto his collar. "Would you like 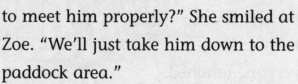 to meet him properly?" She smiled at Zoe. "We'll just take him down to the paddock area."

They all followed Mandy out of the kennels, and Pippin danced around excitedly.

"He's a Jack Russell," Mandy told them as they walked out into the paddock.

"They're very lively little dogs. His mum had a whole lot of puppies and her owners couldn't afford to keep them. We found homes for all the others, but Pippin was the smallest one." Mandy bent down and unclipped Pippin's lead, and the tiny dog scampered off.

Zoe looked at the adorable little puppy, who was running around excitedly, then stared at the adults. "So because he was the smallest no one wanted him?" she asked indignantly.

"Well, no one has yet . . ." Mandy said.

"*Rruff!*" Pippin barked happily as he ran. *How could anyone not want him?* Zoe thought.

Aaron and Leo found a ball, and started kicking it to each other. Pippin crouched down and panted excitedly as he watched them, his head turning from side to side as his eyes followed its movement.

"I think he wants to play!" Zoe laughed.

"Here, boy!" Aaron patted his leg and Pippin raced over to him. Aaron picked up the ball and Pippin immediately plonked down on his bum.

"Did you see that? He sat!" Aaron grinned.

"Come on, boy," Aaron said as he threw the ball across the paddock. Pippin raced off after it, his tiny paws skidding on the ground, then galloped back with the ball clamped tightly in his little mouth.

"Brilliant!" Aaron said. "I bet we can teach him to do loads of tricks." He reached down to take the ball, but Pippin wouldn't let it go. He darted backwards, then ran round Aaron's legs and came over to Zoe. He dropped the ball in

front of her and looked up with a puppy grin. Zoe bent down and gave him a hug, and his tail wagged happily.

"That's the biggest smile I've ever seen," Dad laughed, giving Zoe's hand a squeeze. "He's a lovely dog, isn't he?"

Zoe nodded. "Could he really be ours, Dad?" she asked.

"Yes, if he's the one we definitely want," Dad told her. "It's a big decision. We can think about it for a bit."

Zoe could think about it for ever and Pippin would still be the one she wanted!

Pippin Comes Home

"And then everyone agreed that Pippin was the most perfect dog ever, and now he's going to be *mine*!" Zoe told Maya as they sat in the corner of the playground on Monday.

"That's so amazing!" Maya grinned.

"Well, I have to share him a *bit* with Leo and Aaron and Mum and Dad," Zoe said honestly. "But *I'm* going to love him the most."

Maya sighed. "I wish I was allowed a dog."

"You can come and see Pippin whenever you like," Zoe promised. "I'll ask Mum if you can come round as soon as we get him."

Maya whooped with excitement. "That would be amazing! When can he come home?"

"A lady from Battersea Dogs & Cats Home has to come round first to check everything is OK for a puppy," Zoe explained. "They've got to do that to make sure that there's enough room and it's safe and everything."

"But your house is really big," Maya said, puzzled.

"Yeah, but they don't know that –
that's why they check," Zoe told her.
"Anyway, Mum says there's so much
room, we shouldn't let Pippin go upstairs
for a little while, until he gets used to the
house. Otherwise he'll get lost!" Zoe
giggled.

"What are you
laughing at, Shortie?"
a horrible voice
came from nearby.
Mark was walking
past with his friends.

"Just ignore him,"
Maya told Zoe.

But Zoe was far too
happy to worry about him. "Today I
don't care what Mark says about my
height." She grinned. "When I think
about Pippin I feel like I'm ten foot tall!"

*

Zoe gasped as she heard the *beep* of a car
horn, and a familiar, "*Rruff! Rruff!*"

"Dad's back!" She whooped with
excitement. "Aaron, Leo, Mum! Dad's
back with Pippin!"

Zoe rushed out of the house just as her
dad was getting out of the car. He
was holding a long blue lead,
and on the other end of it
was her puppy! Pippin
ran straight up to her,
his tail wagging
excitedly.

"Hi, Pippin!" Zoe grinned, bending down to stoke him. "I think you've grown!"

Pippin sniffed all round her, his ears pricked, and gave a happy *"Rruff!"*

Mum, Aaron and Leo all came out and made a fuss of the little pup. Pippin ran from one person to the next, his tail wagging madly.

"Welcome home, Pippin!" Zoe grinned.

"Do you want to take him in?" Dad offered.

Zoe nodded as she took the lead. "This way, Pippin," she called, leading the excited puppy over to the open front door. Pippin scrambled up the steps and ran inside.

Dad shut the door firmly behind him, and Mum closed the gate they'd set up at the bottom of the stairs. It had been up in the loft ever since Zoe was little, but Mum had said it was a good way to make sure that Pippin only went in the lounge and the kitchen for a while.

"OK, you can let him off his lead now," Mum said.

Leo and Aaron rushed to help, but Zoe got there first. She unclipped Pippin's lead, expecting the little puppy to run around. But he just looked up at her curiously.

"Go and explore!" Zoe laughed. "This is your doggy flap." She pointed to the new square in the back door. Pippin went over and sniffed it.

"Open it in case he wants to go outside and do his business," Mum said. "It's been a long car journey for a little pup."

Zoe flipped the catch on the dog flap, and Pippin came over curiously to see what she was doing. He peered outside, but he didn't seem to want to go out. Instead he looked at Zoe and gave a doggy grin.

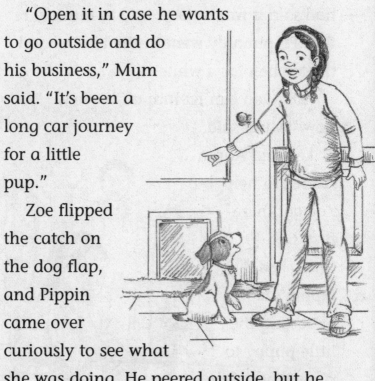

"I know what'll make him move," Leo said. He disappeared into the kitchen, and seconds later there was a rattling sound as he shook the dry puppy food they'd bought. Pippin shot into the kitchen as fast as his little legs would carry him!

Everyone followed, giggling, and watched as Pippin started nibbling on the dry food. He crunched some up happily, then looked around the kitchen as if he was saying, *What's next?*

"In here is your basket," Zoe said, going into the lounge. Pippin padded after her.

Zoe knelt down and patted the soft cushion. Pippin gave it a good sniff, then jumped onto it happily. "Mum says that you have to sleep in the lounge," Zoe whispered to him, "but you can sleep at the end of my bed if you want."

"I heard that!" Mum called.

For the rest of the afternoon, Zoe
rushed around delightedly. Everywhere
she went, Pippin followed. When the time
came to say goodnight, Zoe felt really
bad about going up the stairs and
shutting the stair gate.

"He'll be fine,"
Mum said. "He's
got everything he
needs right here."
But when Zoe got
into bed she
could hear Pippin
whining.

She lay there
and listened as
Mum and Dad came
up to bed. Finally the music
from Leo's room stopped. Then she heard

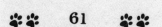

another whine from the bottom of the
stairs. *Pippin was still awake too!*

Zoe climbed out of bed and crept
downstairs, dragging her duvet
after her.

Pippin was sitting
next to the stair
gate, looking up
sadly. As soon as
he saw Zoe he
jumped up and his
tail started wagging.
It was just like the first
time she'd seen him at
Battersea Dogs & Cats Home!

Zoe opened the stair gate and gave
Pippin an enormous hug. "Mum said you
couldn't sleep in my room," she
whispered into his fur. "But she didn't say
I couldn't stay down here with you!"

She lay down on the sofa and wrapped herself up in her duvet. Pippin jumped up next to her and snuggled in. Zoe's thumb went to her mouth, but then she took it out and put her arm over Pippin instead. She hugged his warm, furry body and shut her eyes, feeling happier than she'd ever been before.

Pippin's Adventure

"He's *so* gorgeous!" Maya cried as Zoe opened the front door with Pippin in her arms.

The next day, it was time for Pippin's first walk, and Mum had let Maya come round specially to meet him. Mum had been really surprised when she'd found Zoe sleeping on the sofa, but she'd said that Zoe and Pippin had looked so cute curled up together that she couldn't be cross!

"Don't take your shoes off," Zoe said as Maya came in. "Then we can go straight away – as soon as my brothers are ready."

"OK," Maya agreed excitedly. Zoe put her boots on and sat on the sofa impatiently. Pippin sat at their feet, holding his lead in his mouth.

Mum giggled when she saw them and took a photo with her phone. "You three are so sweet," she told them. "Leo, Aaron!" she called up the stairs. "We're taking Pippin out!"

There was a clattering sound as the boys thumped down the stairs. "Walk!" Mum yelled up at them.

"Yeah, we know, Mum. We're taking Pippin for a walk," Leo said cheekily.

Zoe rolled her eyes and Maya giggled.

Finally they all set off for the park. Zoe had to take turns with Maya, Leo and Aaron at holding his lead, but she didn't take her eyes off Pippin for a second. When it was her turn to hold him, she giggled as the tiny puppy pulled her along. There were fallen leaves all over the path, and Pippin went from one to the next as if he was going to sniff every single one!

After a while
Aaron and Leo
ran ahead,
kicking a ball to
each other
through the
leaves, but Zoe
and Maya walked
along with Pippin.
Zoe felt really grown up,
taking her very own dog for a walk.

"Can we unclip his lead?" Maya
asked, looking at the other dogs running
around.

"No, not yet," Dad replied. "We won't
let him off his lead for a while, until he's
used to us. If he went off now he wouldn't
know to come back!"

Zoe had never noticed how many dogs
there were in the park before. There were

spotty ones and furry ones, dirty ones covered with mud and tiny ones that ladies carried around with them, but none of them were as nice as Pippin. Zoe really liked it when they went past another person with a dog, because the dog walker always said hello and the dogs gave each other a friendly sniff.

Walking with her best friend, her family and Pippin, Zoe didn't think she could get any happier. She felt a huge smile spread across her face, and kicked up some leaves merrily.

"That's a BIG dog!" Maya interrupted her thoughts.

Zoe looked up. Coming towards them was a man with a huge dog – he was almost as big as Zoe was! Zoe gulped and pulled Pippin close. Pippin pulled on his lead, trying to go over to the dog, and then turned round to look at Zoe questioningly.

"Hold on, Pippin," Zoe said, looking round to ask her mum and dad what to do.

But as she turned, Dad called, "Look out!" A cyclist sped right past Zoe, her bell, and she fell over. "Aargh," she cried as she stumbled, waving her arms – and dropped Pippin's lead.

Pippin gave an excited *"Rruff!"* and bounded straight up to the big dog, his blue lead trailing after him.

"Pippin!" Zoe called in terror. "Come back!"

Pippin Makes a Friend

Zoe gave a sob as Pippin ran away. What
if he was hurt by the big dog, or ran off
and got lost for ever? She scrambled to
her feet and dashed after the puppy.
Mum, Dad and Maya were all running
too, calling Pippin's name.

The tiny pup raced up to the huge dog
and ran around him, barking excitedly.
The big dog looked down at Pippin like
he was a fly buzzing around annoyingly.

He opened his mouth, showing big yellow teeth, and gave a deep *"WOOF!"*

Then, to Zoe's surprise, he reached down and sniffed the little dog happily.

"Pippin!" Zoe called as she got closer, and he turned and gave her a *"Rruff,"* like he was asking, *Are you looking for me?*

Zoe raced over and grabbed the end of Pippin's lead. Then she bent down and scooped the little dog into her arms. "You scared me so much!" she sobbed into his fur. Mum, Dad and Maya arrived, panting behind her.

"It's all right," Mum said, putting her arms around Zoe and Pippin. "It's OK, no harm done. But perhaps we'd better head home. That's enough excitement for one day!"

Zoe held tightly to Pippin's lead as Mum called the boys and told them what had happened.

"Pippin's so brave!" Leo said admiringly.

"I don't think he knows he's only little," Dad joked as they headed home. "He thinks he's the same size as that Great Dane!"

Soon Zoe couldn't remember what life had been like without a little brown-and-white puppy following her around. The best thing of all was that Pippin seemed to like her more than her brothers. He liked playing in the garden with them, especially tug-of-war with a knotted rope toy they'd got him, but whenever Zoe was home from school, Pippin followed her

everywhere. When they watched TV in
the evenings he sat curled up at her feet,
and even though Mum said it wasn't
allowed and told him off whenever she
found him there, he kept sneaking
upstairs to sleep on the end of Zoe's bed.
He even tried to follow Zoe into the
bathroom!

Weekends were the best times, because
she could spend all
day with Pippin.
On Saturday,
she spent the
morning
lying on
her bed
doing her
homework,
with Pippin
curled up next to her.

When Mum called
them all for lunch,
Pippin sat under
the table while
the boys secretly
fed him bits of
chicken.

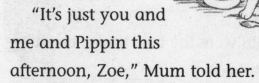

"It's just you and
me and Pippin this
afternoon, Zoe," Mum told her.

"Unless you'd like to come to the
football?" Dad offered. Zoe made a face.

"Come on, Ful-ham!" Leo and Aaron
started to chant. "Come on, Ful-ham!"

Pippin scrabbled at her leg and Zoe
pushed her chair back so that the little
puppy could jump up onto her lap. He
rested his chin on the table and looked
longingly at the chicken that was left on
Zoe's plate.

"What shall we do this afternoon, Pippin?" Zoe asked, fiddling with his little ears. "Hmmm . . . we could watch a film, or play a game – or would you like to go for a walk?" Pippin's ears pricked up when he heard the word "walk", and he turned to face Zoe, panting wildly.

"Walk?" Zoe asked.

"*Rruff!*" Pippin replied excitedly.

"I think Pippin wants to go for a walk, Mum," Zoe giggled.

"*Rruff, rruff!*" Pippin agreed. He jumped down from Zoe's lap in one bound, then came back a second later, with his blue lead in his mouth. The whole family burst into laughter.

"Clever boy!" Zoe got down from her seat and started stroking him. Pippin wagged his tail and rolled onto his back so that Zoe could rub his tummy, but he kept the lead tightly in his mouth.

"You're such a smart puppy!" Zoe giggled.

As Dad and the boys drove off to the football match, Mum, Zoe and Pippin walked round to the park. Mum was

carrying her book, and Zoe was holding
Pippin by his lead and had a ball for
them to play with. Pippin led them to the
park, trotting proudly through all the
leaves.

When they got there, Mum sat on a
bench and started reading, and Zoe
walked Pippin over to a nice grassy hill,
then bent down to unclip his lead. She
wasn't worried about losing him any
more, because she knew Pippin would
come whenever she called.

As she fiddled with his collar, Zoe put
the ball down and it rolled
away. Pippin raced
after it.

"Come back, I haven't taken your lead off yet!" Zoe giggled as the puppy streaked away, dragging his lead behind him.

"Nice dog!" came a familiar horrid voice from behind her. Zoe turned round to see Mark standing there with Alex and Ben. "Or should I say, nice *hamster*."

Zoe's heart sank. She was having such a nice time with Pippin. *Was Mark going to ruin everything?*

The Cowardly Bully

Mark stared at Zoe and Pippin, his lips twisted into a thin smirk. Alex and Ben laughed.

Zoe looked over at her mum, but her head was still bent over her book. She felt a rush of air as Pippin hurried close to her side and dropped the ball at her feet. The ball rolled down towards Mark and he kicked it so hard that it bounced down the hill into some bushes.

Zoe looked down at Pippin, but he didn't run after it. Instead he was sitting really close to her feet, staring at Mark with his ears back.

"That dog is the smallest, stupidest dog I've ever seen," Mark sneered. "A silly little dog for a silly little girl."

Zoe felt like she was about to cry. *How could Mark be so horrible about Pippin?*

"Here, dog," Mark called, patting his

legs as he stepped towards them. "Here, stupid little dog."

Zoe stepped in front of Pippin protectively. But as Mark came nearer, there was a low, cross noise from her feet. Pippin was growling!

Zoe had never heard Pippin make a noise like that before. He was usually so friendly to everyone! "Grrrrrrrrrrr," he growled, showing Mark his teeth fiercely. "Grrrrrr, rruff! Rruff!"

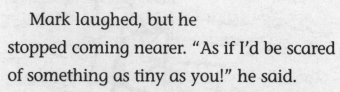

Mark laughed, but he stopped coming nearer. "As if I'd be scared of something as tiny as you!" he said.

"Rruff," Pippin barked, then jumped up and raced towards Mark.

"Pippin!" Zoe called in a panic. But the little dog raced through Mark's legs and then ran back around him again.

"What's he doing?" Mark asked, turning to look at the puppy. He took a step forward, and tripped over Pippin's lead, which was wrapped around his legs!

Mark fell on his bum with a *bump*, and landed right in a muddy puddle! Pippin gave a big growl, and Mark gave a frightened squeak. "Call him off!" he yelled. "Don't let him near me!"

His friends started
laughing at him. Zoe
couldn't help
giggling too, and
Pippin let out a
happy *"Rruff!"*
Pippin dragged his
lead away from
Mark's legs and ran
back over to Zoe, who bent
down and hugged him tightly.

As she looked at her brave little puppy
Zoe felt her heart swell with pride. If
Pippin wasn't afraid of anything, she
shouldn't be either.

Before she could feel scared, Zoe put
Pippin down and walked over to where
Mark was still lying on the ground. She
looked down at him and crossed her
arms. "We might be small, but I'd rather

be small than mean
and horrible like
you!" Zoe shouted.
"I'm not going to
listen to you ever
again, so go away
and STOP calling us
names."

"*Rruff, RRUFF!*" Pippin agreed.

"And if you don't," Zoe added, "I'll tell everyone how you were scared of a tiny dog. Then everyone will know that *you're* the real baby. Come on, Pippin," she finished.

"*Grrrrrrrrrrrr.*" Pippin looked at Mark and gave one last growl, then turned to Zoe. She picked him up, her heart beating fast against his tiny warm body, and walked over towards her mum without looking back.

"We did it, Pippin!" Zoe whispered into his fur, and kissed his little head. Pippin's tail wagged. "And it's all thanks to you. I'd still be scared of him if you hadn't shown me that being small is just as good as being big."

"Are you OK, Zoe?" Mum called as they got closer to her bench. "Was that the boy who was being horrible to you?"

"Yes." Zoe smiled. "But I don't think he'll do it any more. It's nothing that Pippin and I can't handle."

"*Rruff!*" agreed Pippin. "*Rruff, rruff, RRUFF!*"

Read on for lots more . . .

❀ ❀ ❀ ❀

Battersea Dogs & Cats Home

Battersea Dogs & Cats Home is a charity that aims never to turn away a dog or cat in need of our help. We reunite lost dogs and cats with their owners; when we can't do this, we care for them until new homes can be found for them; and we educate the public about responsible pet ownership. Every year the Home takes in around 9,000 dogs and cats. In addition to the site in southwest London, the Home also has two other centres based at Old Windsor, Berkshire, and Brands Hatch, Kent.

The original site in Holloway

History

The Temporary Home for Lost and Starving Dogs was originally opened in a stable yard in Holloway in 1860 by Mary Tealby after she found a starving puppy in the street. There was no one to look after him, so she took him home. She was so worried about the other dogs wandering the streets that she opened the Temporary Home for Lost and Starving Dogs. The Home was established to help to look after them all and find them new owners.

Sadly Mary Tealby died in 1865, aged sixty-four, and little more is known about her, but her good work was continued. In 1871 the Home moved to its present site in Battersea, and was renamed the Dogs' Home Battersea.

Some important dates for the Home:

1883 – Battersea start taking in cats.

1914 – 100 sledge dogs are housed at the Hackbridge site, in preparation for Ernest Shackleton's second Antarctic expedition.

1956 – Queen Elizabeth II becomes patron of the Home.

2004 – Red the Lurcher's night-time antics become world famous when he is caught on camera regularly escaping from his kennel and liberating his canine chums for midnight feasts.

2007 – The BBC broadcast *Animal Rescue Live* from the Home for three weeks from mid-July to early August.

2012 – Paul O'Grady's hit ITV1 series and Christmas Special, *For the Love of Dogs*, follows the stories of many Battersea dogs.

The process for re-homing a dog or a cat

When a lost dog or cat arrives, Battersea's Lost Dogs & Cats Line works hard to try to find the animal's owners. If, after seven days, they have not been able to reunite them, the search for a new home can begin.

The Home works hard to find caring, permanent new homes for all the lost and unwanted dogs and cats.

Dogs and cats have their own characters and so staff at the Home will spend time getting to know every dog and cat. This helps decide the type of home the dog or cat needs.

There are three stages of the re-homing process at Battersea Dogs & Cats Home. Battersea's re-homing team wants to find you the perfect pet: sometimes this can take a while, so please be patient while we search for your new friend!

1 Register details

2 Match

3 Leaving with your new pet

Have a look at our website:
http://www.battersea.org.uk/dogs/ rehoming/index.html for more details!

Fingerprint dogs and cats.

Thumb print over corner of scrap paper and remove to leave white triangle for nose and mouth.

Stick-on eyes: Hole-punched pieces of paper with dots marked in the centres.

Or use white paint to make eyes and tummy.

Making a Mask

Copy these faces onto a piece of paper and ask an adult to help you cut them out.

Jokes

WARNING – you might get serious belly-ache after reading these!

What do you get when you cross a dog and a phone?
A golden receiver!

What is a vampire's favourite dog?
A bloodhound!

What kind of pets lie around the house?
Car-pets!

What's worse than raining cats and dogs?
Hailing elephants!

What do you call a dog that is a librarian?
A hush-puppy!

What do you get when you cross a mean dog and a computer?
A mega-bite!

Why couldn't the Dalmatian hide from his pal?
Because he was already spotted!

What do you do with a blue Burmese?
Try and cheer it up!

Why did the cat join the Red Cross?
Because she wanted to be a first-aid kit!

What happened to the dog that ate nothing but garlic?
His bark was much worse than his bite!

What do you get if you cross a dog with a Concorde?
A jet-setter!

What do you call a cat that has swallowed a duck?
A duck-filled fatty puss!

Did you hear about the cat that drank five bowls of water?
He set a new lap record!

Did you hear about the cat that swallowed a ball of wool?
She had mittens!

Dos and Don'ts of looking after dogs and cats

Dogs dos and don'ts

DO

- Be gentle and quiet around dogs at all times – treat them as you would like to be treated.
- Have respect for dogs.

DON'T

- Sneak up on a dog – you could scare them.
- Tease a dog – it's not fair.
- Stare at a dog – dogs can find this scary.
- Disturb a dog who is sleeping or eating.

- Assume a dog wants to play with you. Just like you, sometimes they may want to be left alone.
- Approach a dog who is without an owner as you won't know if the dog is friendly or not.

Cats dos and don'ts

DO
- Be gentle and quiet around cats at all times.
- Have respect for cats.
- Let a cat approach you in their own time.

DON'T
- Stare at a cat as they can find this intimidating.

- Tease a cat – it's not fair.
- Disturb a sleeping or eating cat – they may not want attention or to play.
- Assume a cat will always want to play. Like you, sometimes they want to be left alone.

Some fun pet-themed puzzles!

Common Dog Breeds

Here is a list of some common dog breeds. See if you can find them in the word search. The words can be written backwards, diagonally, forwards, up and down, so look carefully and GOOD LUCK!

AMERICAN
BULLDOG
BEAGLE
DOBERMAN
GERMAN
SHEPHERD
GREYHOUND
JACK RUSSELL
AKITA
LABRADOR
LURCHER
MONGREL
ROTTWEILER
HUSKY
BULL TERRIER
SHIH TZU
SHAR PEI
BULLMASTIFF

Can you think of any other breeds? Write them in the spaces below

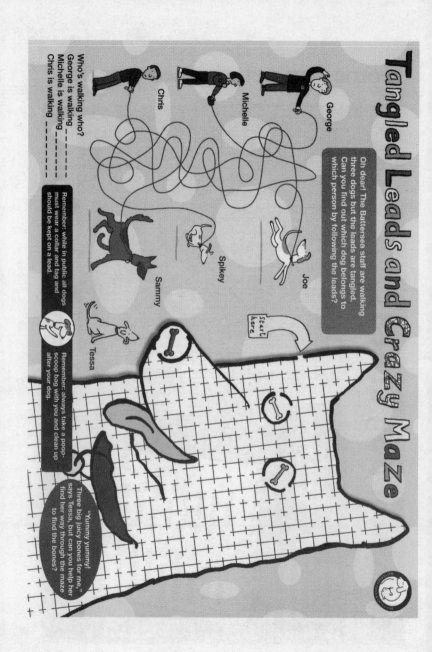

Tangled Leads and Crazy Maze

Oh dear! The Battersea staff are walking three dogs but the leads are tangled. Can you find out which dog belongs to which person by following the leads?

George

Michelle

Chris

Joe

Spikey

Sammy

Tessa

Who's walking who?
George is walking _ _ _ _ _ _ _
Michelle is walking _ _ _ _ _ _ _
Chris is walking _ _ _ _ _ _ _

Remember: while in public all dogs must wear a collar and tag and should be kept on a lead.

Remember: always take a poop-scoop bag with you and clean up after your dog.

start here

"Yummy yummy! Three big juicy bones for me," says Tessa, but can you help her find her way through the maze to find the bones?

108

Drawing dogs and cats

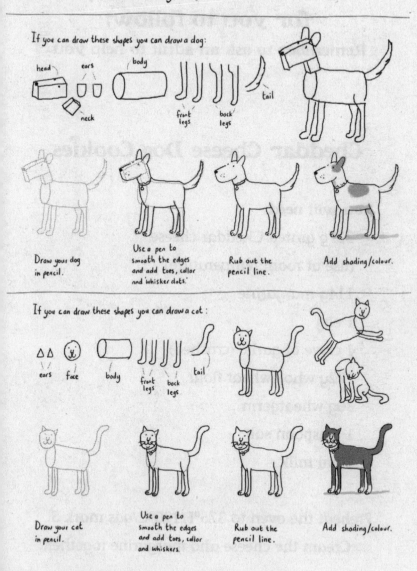

If you can draw these shapes you can draw a dog:

head   ears   body
neck
front legs   back legs   tail

Draw your dog in pencil.

Use a pen to smooth the edges and add toes, collar and 'whisker dots.'

Rub out the pencil line.

Add shading/colour.

If you can draw these shapes you can draw a cat:

ears   face   body   front legs   back legs   tail

Draw your cat in pencil.

Use a pen to smooth the edges and add toes, collar and whiskers.

Rub out the pencil line.

Add shading/colour.

Here is a delicious recipe for you to follow:

Remember to ask an adult to help you.

Cheddar Cheese Dog Cookies

You will need:

227g grated Cheddar cheese

(use at room temperature)

114g margarine

1 egg

1 clove of garlic (crushed)

172g wholewheat flour

30g wheatgerm

1 teaspoon salt

30ml milk

Preheat the oven to 375°F/190°C/gas mark 5.

Cream the cheese and margarine together.

When smooth, add the egg and garlic and mix well. Add the flour, wheatgerm and salt. Mix well until a dough forms. Add the milk and mix again.

Chill the mixture in the fridge for one hour.

Roll the dough onto a floured surface until it is about 4cm thick. Use cookie cutters to cut out shapes.

Bake on an ungreased baking tray for 15–18 minutes.

Cool to room temperature and store in an airtight container in the fridge.

There are lots of fun things on the website, including an online quiz, e-cards, colouring sheets and recipes for making dog and cat treats.

www.battersea.org.uk